STAR WARS

OBI-123

• GALACTIC BASIC EDITION •

WRITTEN BY **CALLIOPE GLASS** & **CAITLIN KENNEDY**
ILLUSTRATED BY **KATIE COOK**

DISNEP

LUCASFILM
P R E S S

Los Angeles · New York

Printed in the United States of America

First Edition, February 2017   10 9 8 7 6 5 4 3 2

Library of Congress Control Number on file

FAC-038091-17258

ISBN 978-1-4847-6812-9

Visit the official *Star Wars* website at: www.starwars.com.

SUSTAINABLE FORESTRY INITIATIVE

Certified Sourcing

www.sfiprogram.org

SFI-00993

Logo Applies to Text Stock Only

ONE
ᗰ∧∧ᐯ

The Jedi had a legend,
An ancient one, of course,
That told of a special someone
Who would bring balance to the Force.
Not a handful of chosen somebodies,
Not a few, not a bunch, not a ton.
Just a single particular Skywalker.
Just Anakin. Just **one**.

TWO

A desert planet on the Outer Rim,
Tatooine is dusty, gritty, and grim.
Everything's parched and thirsty and dry,
From the searing earth to the glaring sky.
Why? you may ask.
Oh, how can this be?
Just look up to the sky,
And you will soon see.
It's those **two** blasted suns,
All round and white-hot.
They're to blame for this heat . . .
But, oh, what a shot!

3 THREE
ヨ7 VI VI

The galaxy is full of remarkable creatures,
Amazing, beautiful, and rare.
But rathtars are just plain awful
(Despite their obvious flair).
These tentacled beasts do only one thing,
And that's gobble up whatever's in sight.
So with **three** of them now on the loose,
Rey and Finn are in for a fight.

4 FOUR
ᱺ᱐᱖᱗

With his **four** metal arms, all whirling and twirling,
General Grievous can fight any foe.
This sinister cyborg is feared through the galaxy.
He's someone you don't want to know.
But even his four spinning sabers of light
Are no match for Obi-Wan's prowess.
In a deadly duel the Jedi at last
Puts an end to Grievous's malice.

FIVE
⻏1Y VI

Over the snowy horizon of Hoth,
Five Imperial walkers appear.
They're mechanical monsters,
Mighty machines
(Even wampas know to steer clear).
But brave Luke Skywalker has a plan
To end these Imperial gimmicks.
As it turns out, defeating an AT-AT
Just takes a little physics.

6 SIX
ↇ1△

The floating cloud city above Bespin
Is home to many a strange creature,
Including the little Ugnaughts–
Whose noses are not their best feature.
But these **six** ugly Ugnaughts sure know their stuff,
And *that* is why they've been chosen
To perform a key task for the Empire:
To make sure Han gets frozen.

7 SEVEN

The Mos Eisley cantina
Is not the greatest gig around.
The crowd is pretty rowdy,
And lost limbs litter the ground.
But these **seven** musicians
Are just looking to jam,
So they'll answer any ad.
And when the Modal Nodes
Play their cheery tune,
The cantina doesn't seem so bad.

EIGHT
Ⅵ 1 Ⅼ7 ☰ ↓

Eight little Jawas, all in a pack,
Excited by their loot—
For finding treasure on Tatooine
Is by far no easy pursuit.
So they carry it along, over the dunes
And across the white-hot sand.
Don't blame them; that's just what it takes
To get by in this desolate land.

NINE

Amidala, queen of Naboo,

Had **nine** handmaidens,

Loyal and true.

Eight were selected

To keep *one* protected.

The queen was disguised as one, too!

10 TEN
↓⋁ᴦ⋂

Imperial officers numbering **ten**
All sat around a big table.
There wasn't a lot that could scare those bad men,
But that day, Darth Vader was able.
The Imperial officers didn't agree
On the best way to beat the Alliance.
So Darth Vader decided to make them all see
That he didn't enjoy their defiance.
Using his powers, he squeezed one of the ten
Quickly into submission.
His goal was to demonstrate clearly to them
That the Force was no "ancient religion."

11 ELEVEN
ᐱᒐ ᒎᐱᒐ Ꭹ ᐱᒐᐱ

Eleven X-wings led by Poe Dameron
Skillfully fly into battle.
They're attacking TIE fighters
And the Starkiller base,
And the structure is starting to rattle.
With one final shot
The Resistance succeeds,
And the planet is gone in a flash.
But the blinding white glow
Simply lights up
The pilots' victorious dash.

12. TWELVE
Ɐ□ⱱⱯΥⱱ

In the days of old, the Jedi stood
For all that was noble, strong, and good.
Steeped in the Force
And wise beyond years,
The Jedi quieted everyone's fears.
Leading this army of virtuous teachers
Was the Jedi Council, a wide range of creatures.
Twelve individuals of all different species
Would meet and discuss various treaties.
On the last Jedi Council before their great fall,
Sat short little Yoda and Windu the tall,
And ten of their cleverest brothers and sisters.
Alas, they're now spoken of only in whispers.

13 THIRTEEN
ヨ17↓Ⅵ Ⅵ ⅥⅣ

Silent, giant ships in dust
Like ancient mountains standing.
Rey weaves her way through all **thirteen**,
Her sharp eyes always scanning.
She's searching for parts to sell or to trade
For a day's portion of food,
Through X-wings and V-wings and fallen Destroyers,
A long-lost multitude.

14 FOURTEEN

Lumbering, wheezing, huge and hairy,
These **fourteen** banthas are far from scary.
Sure, they are smelly
And not very clean.
But they're oh so helpful,
So who needs hygiene?

15 FIFTEEN
ᚦᛁᚠᛏᛖᛖᚾ

On Endor's small forest moon,
The Ewoks prepare for war,
With slingshots and trip lines,
And *possibly* land mines.
The Empire has no idea what's in store.
A group of **fifteen** takes out its wrath
On a slew of white-armored thugs.
All on their own, with no help at all,
The Ewoks crush them like bugs.
Not bad for little furballs,
You've got to give them credit.
After all, they saved the Rebellion,
And the galaxy won't soon forget it.

16 SIXTEEN
ᑎ1ᐃ᙮ ᐑᐑᑎ

A Jedi and a Padawan
Clutch their weapons tight.
They've been training all their lives for this.
They're bracing for a fight.
Sixteen battle droids attack
With heavy blaster fire.
But for Obi-Wan and Qui-Gon Jinn,
It's really not so dire.

17 SEVENTEEN
ᐯᐯᓏᐯᐯᓏᐯ

Seventeen Gamorrean guards
Line a hallway in Jabba's palace.
Tusked and green and horned and mean,
They're as gross as Jabba is callous.
One thing is for sure, these guys are glad
To be guarding this particular aisle.
Their friend had a job near the rancor,
But they haven't seen *him* for a while.

18
EIGHTEEN

The crowds have arrived.

The stands are packed.

They're ready for a show.

Eighteen podracers power up.

A gong rings out.

They're ready to go.

Anakin has a faulty start,

But then he's off with a blast.

Through the desert

He zips and weaves.

He's in the lead at last.

Not even Sebulba's dirty tricks

Can keep Anakin's fate at bay.

He was always meant to win, you see.

The Force is strong with him, they say.

19 NINETEEN
ᘉᓑᘉ ᐯᒣᓑᓇᓇᐯᘉ

Nineteen patrons fill Maz's castle,

And, oh, what an interesting mix.

Thieves and pirates,

Smugglers and spies,

All visiting for kicks.

Just don't step out of line here, folks.

Maz Kanata is the judge.

She's lived for over a thousand years.

You don't want her holding a grudge.

20 TWENTY

Stormtroopers travel in packs of **twenty**,
In transports to be precise.
The transports aren't so comfortable,
But most stormtroopers aren't so nice.
When the heavy ships land,
The troopers inside race right into battle.
But one of them doesn't seem eager to be there.
FN-2187 looks a bit rattled.
The stormtroopers do as they're told.
Nineteen of the twenty dive in.
But the one who stands apart from it all
Is the one who will soon be called Finn.

You disappoint me.
We're at the end of the book, and not once did you count Dooku!

CALLIOPE GLASS

Calliope Glass is a children's book writer and editor in New York City. Her favorite *Star Wars* character is Mon Mothma. She likes to solve crossword puzzles, read comic books, and sing very loudly.

CAITLIN KENNEDY

Caitlin Kennedy lives in San Francisco with her husband, mere miles from the redwoods that inspired the forests of Endor. She has yet to see an Ewok.

KATIE COOK

Katie Cook is an illustrator and writer who has been creating work for *Star Wars* professionally for almost a decade, and unprofessionally with crayons since the mid-1980s. She lives in Michigan with her husband, her daughters, and lots of *Star Wars* toys . . . er, collectibles.